I0451520

Sleazy Shot

Present Day and Time!

By

Jacob Tim Gillanders

Acknowledgments

Special thanks to Ryan King, Judy R, Joshua Graham, Jacob Homberg, Alpha House Staff, Jordan Anderson, Toronto Police, Tucker Gillanders and Crystal Jones.

Table of Contents

Prologue

"Oh, O'Conner, if you had just listened to me and stayed home when the investigation began, you wouldn't be in this… awful predicament. Such a shame. You were so loyal, so hardworking, but also too good-spirited for this division."

"You won't get away with this bullshit game you're pulling," Jack shouted, hoping someone, anywhere, might hear him.

The ground was icy to the touch, a sure sign they were below ground—how deep, Jack couldn't tell. And then, he saw him. Their guy. The mole in all of this.

The missing piece of the puzzle.

Chapter 1:
The Meddling of It All (Simon)

Simon was a happy, smart, and successful student. He was enrolled in Ryerson for Dramatic Arts. With the rising cost of rent, he boarded with his family and remained with them until he graduated. Tall, thick brown hair, his ethnicity grew from Irish to Scottish to West Indian heritage. Tanned skin with a light-creamed coffee color, he could almost make it as a model. Weighing 175 lbs and growing at 5'11'', he was charming and all set for adulthood and what might come of it.

His father was a successful businessman. Ginovvi owned the real estate game with wise investments, financially secure investors, and a business partner who worked alongside Ginovvi for 25 years. The partner also owned several parking lots and a few toll booths across the States.

God gave Ginovvi a gorgeous wife named Shelia Radsonatti, nee Olgswarth. She was independent but loving, compassionate but aggressive.

Simon, their son, was born in Toronto, Ontario, at Mount Sinai Hospital on May 21st, 2008, making him 17 years old next year. He had blue eyes that shimmered like an ice glacier, and with the combination of bleach-blonde hair, he had looks to die for.

Ginovvi was more of a husky man himself, rounding up to 175 lbs at 5'9'', making him broad and muscular. Born on the west coast of Surrey, BC, Canada, on August 27th, 1975, he had ocean-blue eyes and strawberry-blonde hair.

Sheila was born in Arlen, Texas. She had a curvy chin with boy-like features, green eyes, and a body that just won't quit. Zumba and hot yoga helped, and throw in the cute, light-brown hair on top of baby-like skin, and she was irresistible. Her dad passed away when she was young, and she grew up in Toronto with little income from her mother.

Ginovvi came from an upper middle-class family and had a custom taste in life and its affairs. He even ensured that his profitable shares in the real estate business were over 65% so he could always seize complete control if things took a different turn.

Doug Foreheights, his partner, was a shorter man—5'6" and 210 lbs, to be precise. He had brown eyes and dark brown hair. He was a Toronto local born in Scarborough General Hospital, so he knew the area well.

The real estate business was established in the early 90s, and Doug became a tycoon for North American sales in houses, condos, and commercial properties. They called it Radheights. He did fancy himself to many of the perks of being a co-owner to Radheights, such as black car service 24/7, access to luxurious condos within the GTA, RRSPs, and TFSAs pre-set, health insurance the public didn't have access to, reserved seating at many stadiums and sports fields.

Yes, Ginovvi and Doug truly had it all, with the company's net worth sitting at $78,000,000.00. They would have annual family vacations to exotic countries and tours with the rich at the yacht club on the company yacht. You would think, what more could a person ask for in such an extravagant lifestyle?

To mark a normal day with the real estate clan, Ginovvi and Shelia would wake up together a lot of the time simultaneously. Ginovvi would head straight to the kitchen to grab a coffee and go off to his office. Shelia would wake Simon up and prepare breakfast for the family, check the weather and roads for efficiency, and see news bulletins on her phone. After Simon ate his food and prepared for school, he would head out the door with Shelia, while Ginovvi would head to the work office to consult business.

The day would go by, with Shelia first dropping Simon off at his school, then heading to the supermarket to grab some food that the house usually needed if groceries weren't to be bought. Later, Shelia would hit up her girlfriends and spend a little time at the mall. Lunchtime was usually when Ginovvi and Doug would treat Shelia and some coworkers to lunch if the agenda wasn't overfull. For the afternoon, Shelia headed home after lunch to clean the house and tidy up where needed.

Ginovvi sweated profusely and constantly checked his iPhone, praying to God for a work emergency. He struggled to announce to his wife at Earl's restaurant in downtown Toronto that he was leaving her to be with Doug. Finally, by God, he did it (thankfully, Simon was at a sleepover). Sheila just stared off into the distance as if she hadn't heard a thing or wasn't even conscious.

"YOU'RE LEAVING ME FOR THAT!?" she shouted. "Like, oh my God, Gino, what the fuck am I going to tell Simon when I get home? Oh yeah, your dad decided after all the years he's been with Mommy it's time to FUCK his business buddy, Doug!"

He sighed and covered his face as many other restaurant patrons were staring in curiosity, wondering what ratchet, out-of-control Jerry Springer scene they were about to observe. Sheila got up and excused herself to the bathroom, screaming to the restaurant, "IF ANYONE SAYS ANYTHING TO ME, I'LL PUNCH THE FUCK OUT OF YOU!" She stormed off in a rage to the ladies' room.

Doug wiped his mouth as he was plowing back on the shrimp when Sheila exploded, popcorn to a movie. "Say, Gino, maybe we should move your things to my place while we still can. Is Sheila violent to property or you, or me…?"

Ginovvi shrugged. "Yeah, that would be funny. No, she knows how to play the legal battle of 'how much can I steal,' so I've already had paperwork pre-assigned to take care of any wrongdoings in divorce court."

Doug exhaled as if he had been underwater for twenty seconds. "You think it's over yet?"

The women's bathroom door slammed open. Sheila stomped toward the men with fury in every crevice of her body and face, as if steam lifting from her beet-red forehead. The guys almost shivered at the sight of her, both holding their breath and waiting for her to pounce.

"GINOVVI, you can sleep at Doug's house from now on or wherever the fuck that troll lives. The house is mine. I will hire a lawyer, and we'll be in touch! Oh, and GO FUCK YOURSELF!"

She threw the bread bowl with three buns left at Doug's face. Security was there to escort Ms. Radsonatti outside, but she assuredly took her stance and left the restaurant.

"Well, who called that one, Gino?"

Ginovvi just shook his head in disappointment.

Chapter 2:
New Chief (O'Conner)

Jack O'Conner was promoted to homicide detective about a year ago after working seven hard years on the force. He started as a constable, then was promoted to sergeant, and finally, after finishing his detective course, he became a homicide detective.

He was a newcomer detective but was blessed with wisdom and observation skills as sharp as a cat's! Jack always pointed out details and facts others couldn't see—simple things like subconscious behaviour and verbatim recall of word choices in conversations between parties.

He lived alone after a brutal breakup with a fiancée who later accidentally overdosed. She had been taking medication for seizures and tried psychedelic mushrooms with alcohol after her friend's peer pressured her into it.

Detective Jack O'Conner was 34 years old, born on August 27, 1989, in London, Ontario, Canada. Raised by his mom as a single parent, his father was a wasted crackhead with no conscience or remorse. He was affectionate to those in severe trauma or pain, as he himself carried quite a burden in his subconscious mind. Healthy? Absolutely not! Did he give himself much of a choice? No. In the police field, there's not much time to deal with mental health. O'Conner typically stuck to his routine when it came to a day of work and such—starting with his regular hygiene ritual upon waking up, followed by coffee and breakfast in the kitchen, greeting Skipper (his Great Dane) and pouring high-protein dog food into his shiny steel bowl.

After all that morning magic is done, I start what I call "force prep." I pick formal clothing with no overly strong threads and durable material. Then I throw on my gun jacket (holster), and on goes the blazer. I always keep my badge next to the gun in the nightstand right beside my double bed. It's a lonely life, it seems, but the bills are paid, and I have time and enough funds to vacation here and there. Not to mention the late nights with the team at bars or new restaurants—after a while, even the guys who annoy you start to become like family. It's true that police officers really do care more for one another than for civilians. After a quick cologne spritz and a mirror check, I head to the door, grab my keys, give Skipper one last kiss goodbye, and fly down the staircase of my building's old hallway and structure.

I have been here for eight years now as a detective, and to be frank with you, it feels like it's falling apart faster and faster with each passing minute. It's home because Toronto rent prices have skyrocketed, and I'm grandfathered in here.

The heating is incredibly loud, the hot water barely runs, and the neighbours are more than nosy, but to Jack, it was just home.

He spoiled himself when it came to his ride: a Dodge Charger V8, alloy rims, spoiler, and body kit. It was the next closest thing he had to a child, next to Robbie. A '18 model, all red with black decals on the doors, it was his pride and joy. He truly loved commuting to work; the station was downtown Toronto, while he lived in northwest Etobicoke (16 miles away). Lately, Jack had been getting into certain podcasts; he loved hearing about the next idiot's biggest conspiracy theory or how the world was supposedly meant to end tomorrow. "Bah, what stupid bullshit," he'd think, just there to entertain his ears.

The downtown division recently got a reno done, which was years overdue. The parking lot was state-of-the-art. His key card scanned on entry, and there was a camera with the station guard inside watching 24/7. Driving under the steel overpass always made him nervous about bringing in his Escalade (his summer car). The clearance read 6'1" when he knew his true baby stood up to 6'8" (with spoiler tail). That's why the Charger stayed as his commute car, and the Escalade sat at his mother's up in Barrie, out in the country where its largest threats were snow and coyotes.

Parking space 2A12, with a sign and all nailed to the concrete wall, stating it's my parking spot. Let me tell you, what a pain it is to idle your vehicle as you go upstairs to locate the idiot who didn't follow directions or read the sign right in front of their stupid face. I try to take the stairs more often, even though my office is on the third floor; the doctor has been advising more stair exercise to help blood flow and maintain healthy veins.

So, as I settle into my seat, within 30 seconds in flies the super assistant Janet Clarkson, with memos stuck to her forehead and a 30 lb file binder in her hands, practically weighing the poor girl down to the floor.

She threw it on Jack's desk as if it was about to catch fire. "Watch it, Jan-Jan!" (She hated this name, but since she was crushing on Jack, she let it slide.) "You almost karate-chopped me a file holder."

"Sorry, Jacky," she replied, gasping for air. "I've been a bit tense lately. Branson isn't sleeping right—or sometimes at all. I don't know who the fuck said 'terrible twos', it should be 'sadistic sevens!'"

Jack shuffled through the paper mountain to find the right binders. "Well, the sock strangler is back at it, I see."

Janet gazed at the floor, then remembered she was also assistant to two other detectives, and scurried out into the buzz of people and constant chatter.

Chantelle, the most butch woman to live on planet Earth, was also the Toronto Chief of Police. She entered O'Conner's office and announced her new role as acting chief. Chantelle Robertson was her full name, and she was a bit of a nerd, wearing square-framed glasses. Chantelle moved closer to Jack and shook his hand while the opportunity was there.

"Nice to meet you, hope you're ambitious like me!"

He checked his phone and opened his home security app to see how his beloved Skipper was—probably sleeping on the floor or trying to rip the couch apart. For a Great Dane, he was awfully aggressive and hyper, so for the furniture's sake, Jack checked in often. But of course, Skipper was behaving at home and not ripping all the fabric out of the couch. Jack smiled, put his phone in his pocket, and started reviewing the documents thrown onto his desk moments ago.

Chapter 3:
Bells, Bells Take Me To Hell!
(Shelia)

Her flight to Texas landed in Arlen by 8:03 AM, and she had already prebooked an Uber to her mother's house, not telling her what had happened from the start. Once she landed, retrieved her luggage, and loaded herself into the car, she decided to ring her mom to announce her arrival.

"Hey, Shelia, sweetie, how are you?" Peggy said.

"Well, Mom, I'm here in Texas, and I'm on my way to see you."

Peggy was astonished and surprised to learn her only child was visiting her after so long; the last time she saw her daughter was at Simon's communion.

"Well, what a lovely surprise! I'll get myself ready and tidy up the house before you arrive. Love you!"

Shelia smiled for the first time since the entire incident at the restaurant, where her life had nearly fallen apart.

Shelia had a specific schedule mentally engraved in her brain that she executed from the second she opened her eyes to the minute she slept again. Now that she was living with her mother temporarily and hadn't slept last night, except briefly in the hotel room attached to the airport, her whole schedule was over the place, but so was her life. So, she chugged an espresso and prepared for many hugs, kisses, and random questions; the rewiring of her daily routines was going to take time. Typically, she could adjust to a new rhythm of life in Arlen, Texas, going from Canadian to Southern American. Real fun.

"Fuck my life," Shelia thought to herself, cramped in her mother's guest room with no job, no friends, and no one to talk to. Her mother drove her obnoxiously insane, so she learned a technique: when it became too much for her to handle, she would politely tell her mom she needed "me time" and proceed to another room without dear old mommy. Her mother would distract her with Sudoku game sheets and the TV.

She quickly withdrew her laptop from her luggage and skimmed through Gino's profile to see any horrifying pictures of the new lovebirds. Nope, nothing. Moving on, she googled divorce lawyers, as she didn't want the company lawyer as he wasn't impartial to the entire family. She had met him a few times; he seemed like a sweet man—older, of course—and he was in Mississauga: Danny Martin. She found a few plausible candidates and emailed them; she would use her credit cards to pay them along with what savings she had. She kept a few thousand in separate accounts over the years to surprise her husband with nice gifts, but now that money had a different purpose.

Simon was born, and Ginovvi paid for everything she enjoyed as a woman; even certain products mattered! Shelia had to wonder what the hell those two were going to tell Simon. "Doesn't matter. Girl, you are now taking care of yourself; Simon is 17 months away from being an adult, and with those two fairies running the business, they will be fine. There's going to be a fucking wedding—I can feel it—and let me tell you, I'm going to go there and sabotage the shit out of it." Shelia thought.

She continued scrolling through Gino's social media pages and saw nothing indicating he was gay with his business partner. She started to scan photos and became infuriated with every passing smile. She shut her computer and laid down on the bed, rubbed her eyes, and started to think.

"Will my son call me, or is he going to blame me for leaving him there with his newly found gay dad and his lover? I couldn't really blame him either; this is a totally fucked-up situation for a teenage boy, and his mother just flew away like some fucking pigeon. What a sad woman I am. Pondering that led me to think of ways to surprise my soon-to-be adult son. Maybe a car—well, I'd have to get a loan. I'll die before I ever ask for that man for help again. If he's helping me, it's going to be court-ordered or demanded; fuck asking for anything anymore."

Shelia sat up and decided to run herself a bath and search on her phone what kind of gift to give her newly traumatized son. Shelia's mother went by Peg, who was legally named Peggance at birth. Any family members never mention the name; they know the consequences that would come with such actions. Shelia's mother was raised in the prairies her entire childhood and could deliver a can of whup-ass when requested. Stern punishment is how the country folk do things; it is supposed to keep their family members in line and focused on farm work. Yet, abuse like this resulted in suppressed emotions and feelings that turned ugly in senior years. Fortunately for Peg, she kept a clean bill of health and a large netted bank account, thanks to three husbands, all hard-working men who died on her year after year.

"SHELIA! DON'T USE ALL THE HOT WATER NOW!" Flo shouted up the staircase. Ugh, more hillbilly behavior from dear old mom. She set her phone down and propped herself up to shout back, "WOULD YOU SHUT THE FUCK UP? IT'S A BATH, NOT A SHOWER! DO YOU HEAR RUNNING WATER?"

Back to retail shopping through a glowing square, Shelia then received a notification for an email. Her phone was submerged in the bathtub. "THEY REALLY HAD TO PULL THIS SHIT, AHHHHHHHHH!" The bathroom door slammed open, and out came naked, soap-covered, raging Shelia to find her poor old mom, making her the victim of Rant City.

The couple announced on X (formally Twitter) that they were together and that he was filing for divorce. Shelia had decided to treat her mother to an afternoon out at a local restaurant to celebrate the small reunion of the two after several years of being apart due to raising Simon and her failing marriage with Ginovvi. Now that she can truly open up to her mother about how she feels about her marital issues, she is excited about her newfound life.

She didn't seem to remember that her mother struggled with alcohol abuse, and when she chose the spot to eat, there was a drink menu that she had not noticed upon arriving at the diner. Shelia's mom was more than subtle; she was downright stealthy with her every action like any addict would be. After the name of the diner was announced, Peggy tried to find the power to tell her daughter she could not go there due to her possibility of relapse, but unfortunately, the power of the disease overcame her, and she didn't say a word. They drove in their 1998 Honda Civic, which Peggy had properly taken care of, to Madison's Diner and parked behind the restaurant beside a dumpster.

"Hey, Mom, is there anything you noticed between Gino and his business partner, Doug?" Shelia quickly asked as they exited the vehicle. Peggy had a bad hip from old age, so she took her time to respond to the question. "Well, pumpkin, I don't really know what to tell you. I noticed all sorts of odd things about Gino and his behavior, like he never bothered to call me. He never sent any birthday cards to me or your father when he was still around."

Shelia rolled her eyes and restated herself. "No, I mean within the time frame of our wedding and before Simon was born. Was he ever appearing not trustworthy or dishonest? I just feel like that would have been a sign that he was gay and that I should have noticed it. But you know how we women get with weddings and pregnancy. You're not me, so did he appear off or shady to you when you came to Toronto for our wedding?"

They were seated at their table before Peg composed a proper answer that Shelia would accept. Peg was also shocked she had forgotten that the diner served liquor, and she then started planning her secret relapse. She didn't think of it as that yet, but when Peg drinks, she tends to be loud, arrogant, and vulgar.

She would wait for the right opportunity to steal some wine from the kitchen. Shelia ordered iced tea, and her mother decided on coffee. They thoroughly plowed through the bread basket as they hadn't had breakfast due to Shelia's early arrival at the Dallas airport. When only the crumbs remained, Peggy chimed in, "You know, at one point, sugarplum, I heard from Simon that he caught his new stepdad flirting with some local waitress at those fancy cocktail places he would always take you to. But then again, that was five years ago, so maybe he was still in denial about being gay. It's 2024, Shelia. Times are different. Do you think you're the only woman who has kids with a gay man? It's more common than you think."

The waiter came back with lunch menus and napkins for the two southern gals. Shelia was not too hungry after all that bread, and she felt incredibly stupid for mowing down like a starving child from Africa; now, she had wasted so much Zumba and cardio that she wanted to die right in that booth. Caesar salad was the answer. Peggy went ahead and ordered a full steak sandwich, as she wanted to ensure there was food in her stomach in preparation for her fuck-up. She took note of where the waiter would exit the kitchen with food and devised a plan for after her daughter finished her salad.

Peggy wasn't at all conscious of her problems; rather, she had a new fixation on her old, sweet, damaging friend—red wine. Shelia carried on about how Ginovvi never helped Simon as he grew older or when he was a baby and how he never helped with any chores or errands around the house. It was just all very stressful for Shelia to think about, so once it came time for the main entrées to arrive from the kitchen, all the poor woman could do was quietly and secretly sob to herself as her mother peered around the room.

As the meal went on, Peggy excused herself to the bathroom, and then came the plan. She patiently waited as if there was someone in the women's washroom; she checked to make sure the coast was clear in terms of walking into the kitchen. Fortunately, the wine and alcohol fridge was located right by the door in a small room that had a counter for ready-to-go meals and a cupboard above it for cups. Once the waiter had exited, she entered the small room, yanked open the fridge door, and grabbed the first bottle of red wine she saw. She had her purse with her, so she stuck it inside her bag.

Once in the washroom, she took her first chug and kept going—just like that, two years of sobriety were gone.

Chapter 4:
Unveiling (Simon)

When the school bell rang, Simon never anticipated the conversation he was about to have when he got home with his father and his new estranged friend. Like any teenager, all he could think about after school was dinner and how sick he was of geometry. He texted his father about the new iPhone his dad had bought him two days ago. Out of the blue, Simon had asked for a simple flip phone two months back, and the answer had been a direct and fast but harsh "NO." Now, suddenly, his father had bought him a new iPhone.

Something was up; he just couldn't put his finger on what he needed to talk about with his father. Ginovvi texted him on his way home from school. He would hide his admittance to convince the trending phone brand but would always publicly still complain about everything. He arrived 20 minutes later after sitting in back-to-back traffic to see his dad and Doug, his new friend.

Doug was grimmer than Simon expected. Surely, he must do a lot of paperwork on business affairs; his face was not customer-friendly. His dad pulled the Rover up to the curb for high school drop-off. He opened the door and noticed his father was worried about something—the look on his face was pale.

The drive home was quiet, which Simon didn't mind, considering how the conversation tonight might go. He hoped for the best as they turned into the driveway of their three-bedroom home. For some odd reason, he knew Mom had taken off to America to stay with Grandma. He arrived home on the Lakeshore coast of Toronto; it had a cobblestone driveway with a gated entrance.

Once they were all inside the house, you could feel the drama creeping up to the present moment. Simon and Ginovvi sat down at the table for dinner as Doug had promised to cook. That was not the main task; it was explaining why Shelia wasn't there to greet her son.

"So, son, I have something I want to tell you. You can see that Doug is here. Well, I wanted to tell you now for some time that I'm not who you think I am," Ginovvi said as he sweated like a heroin addict.

Simon continued to watch and listen, as this was both entertaining and awkward at the same time. He had known for years.

"It's taken me a long time to come to this conclusion, and I've been hiding it for years to keep your mom happy and you free from ridicule, but Doug, my business partner, is my lover, and I've already left your mother. She quickly went to make arrangements to go south to be with her mother. The flight left yesterday, and I assume she's with her mother now. Simon, I still love you and your mother very much. Just recently, in the past few years, I've discovered more about myself than I ever knew," Ginovvi said.

Doug finally chimed in, "You don't have to consider me your father in any sense. I am not obligating you, but I'm sure we can get along over time. Your father and I have been seeing each other romantically for the past four months."

Simon grunted and walked off to his bedroom. "I think I need some alone time and personal space, do you understand?"

The two men sat alone in the family room, struggling to get up and start cooking dinner. The conversation could carry on later. Simon threw his backpack on the floor and sighed. Hopes that this drama would blow over were long dead. He pulled out his phone and texted his girlfriend—the one bit of sanity in his life—to update her on the events that occurred at his so-called "home."

He went into vivid detail and even dashed out his beliefs for how the evening had gone and what poorly executed "talk" he had with his now newly founded *dads*. The night would surely end at some point, Simon thought to himself. He then decided to call her.

"Hey Angie, want to go see a movie? I heard a really funny comedy was released today," he said, smiling with blushing cheeks.

She responded in a soft tone, "Heya Simon, I'd love to see a movie with you."

Simon packed himself some junk food, as he was cheap and didn't agree with the overpriced food at the theatre. They took public transit to the nearby mini-mall, where they got food from the dollar store and shoved it all into Angie's backpack after purchasing it.

Simon wanted to move things forward regarding the relationship status, so tonight was the perfect opportunity to see where it all stood between them. Angie was 5'9" with yellowish-brown eyes, taller than most girls but still of average height. She was skinny with brunette hair, which she bleached to blonde most of the year. Well-educated and surprisingly athletic, she was the captain of the volleyball team. Ethnically Laotian, her background and character were really interesting for a girl her age, 16.

They made it there just past 9 PM, and the movie had already started, so they rushed into the theater and grabbed a seat at the top, where they preferred to cuddle in privacy. Simon was sweating from anxiety; this was his chance to make a move on his new girlfriend. He didn't want to ruin the relationship they had worked so hard on so far, but she smiled at him a lot and blushed from time to time. So, Simon was pretty sure this would work out just fine.

The credits rolled by, and before they knew it, the Bunker Games began. Simon started sweating already; he had been thinking about Angie all night. She noticed and asked, "Hey Simon, are you okay? You're soaking your shirt!" He laughed and shrugged. "Well, yeah, I just really want tonight to be special because, well, Angie, I have to tell you something. It's hard for me to talk about this stuff, and I don't want to come on too strong, but can my first time be with you, say, after prom?"

Angie blushed and darted back. "I kind of figured. Uhm, I'd have a problem if it was someone else, but let's not plan it. It will happen when it happens." Simon tended to get incredibly sweaty with nerve-racking scenarios, so he kept a few sheets of paper towel in his pocket.

Finally, after long moments of awkwardness, they found themselves finally holding hands.

The ending was bland compared to how they advertised the movie. Even Angie was annoyed because the plot line didn't match the rest of the story, which upset her. They decided to ditch the movie 20 minutes before the credits. They were in hormonal stages and gave in to the temptation; that meant kissing, cuddling, and second-base action at most!

Simon started to become concerned about his mother, as he hadn't received any type of message in the past 72 hours. He whipped up a quick, kindly paragraph (he was always incredibly awkward), sent it off, and returned to giving his attention to Angie. They finally reached the house where Angie lived with her grandparents. It's customary to drop the girl off first to ensure she's safe.

With sweat running down his cheeks, he kissed her goodbye, as this was considered the first date. He didn't know if he was going to be that lucky tonight, but seeing as they were standing in front of the closed front door, he caught the signal.

He went home on a local bike path and gazed through news sections on his phone. His perception of entertainment had changed as he grew closer to being an adult. He also noticed that studying was becoming easier and harder at the same time—with his increasing love of acquiring knowledge, which was the easy part. The difficult part was when he was studying a subject he wasn't interested in.

He arrived home, and his dad was dead asleep while Doug was watching the news. Simon always knew he was gay since he was 7 years old, not from any physical sign, but he came across his father fooling around with a lover at the time. His name was Maxwell. He caught them fucking in his car once at night when Simon strolled out for a walk. It was in an empty parking lot near the beach, so no legal trouble arose.

It was both funny and sad that his father had denied himself for so long; it must have been hard to keep those feelings locked up.

"Hey Simon, how was your movie?" Doug asked quietly, bringing Simon back to the current moment.

"Uh, it was okay. We didn't finish it, sort of sucked, to be honest."

Doug grinned. "Well, have a good sleep. I'm just catching up on the news, as you can see."

Simon went to his room and was curious as to why Doug had stated the obvious. Maybe he thought that Simon smoked weed or was an idiot, which is why he wanted to explain. Nonetheless, Simon was off to bed.

Chapter 5:
New Sheriff, Corner Croaks
(Jack Oconner)

Jack had to hurry to the station that morning, racing into work after his alarm hadn't gone off as usual. He was hitting 140km/h on the highway when he saw the Bay Street exit on the Gardiner Expressway. He zoomed down the ramp, made a quick left turn, and sped up Bay Street, his lateness practically written all over his speedometer.

As he pulled into the underground garage, his Charger nearly hit the clearance post. He slammed the car door shut, ran like a fool to the elevators, and tried to check his emails—but of course, he had no reception underground. For some reason, the elevator music was just radio static.

On the 5th floor of the Toronto Metropolitan Police headquarters, Jack's office and those of other detectives were located. Janet, his colleague, looked particularly perky yet anxious. Jack made a mental note to ask her about it later, but for now, he needed to get the briefing.

His tardiness didn't go unnoticed. The sheriff, who led the briefing, couldn't resist poking fun at him as he entered. "Jack, you're late! This isn't typical behavior. Anyway, there are a few things I wanted to discuss with you." Jack felt the firm grip of Chantelle's hand on his shoulder.

"So, there's been a few rumors spreading about me being gay and Baptist. I don't mind either of those labels. It's just that I go to a Christian United congregation, and I don't want my fellow church members to think I've left their group. If you could maybe try to find out who's been spreading these rumors, I'd really appreciate it. Think of it as a personal job from the top, like you're a secret agent." Jack shrugged and agreed to take on this stupid, gossipy, small-town task to get on her good side since she was new. Chantelle then turned and bolted out of Jack's office.

Back at his desk, he resumed his morning routine. Janet was scrolling through social media when Detective Jack returned. "So, Janet, sorry about Chantelle just pulling me away like that. What's happened so far this morning on my leads?"

Janet quickly rolled to the one side of her desk, rifled through some papers, and handed Jack the morning brief log sheet. "Well, Jack, so far, your leads for case 3215 and case 3422 are still the same. For 3215, witness #2 has no recollection of the entire night (the stabbing that turned into a homicide), and for 3422, we still don't have any witnesses willing to testify yet" (a drug bust). "However, you did get a response from the nurse at Toronto General. She'll accept your dinner invitation. She just requested you pick somewhere away from downtown."

Jack blushed a little at the thought of her accepting. Felicia was an outgoing critical care nurse at Toronto General Hospital. They met when Jack was bringing in a homicide suspect, someone he'd caught who later claimed to be suicidal. Felicia was just about to finish her training with her team and happened to be shadowing the nurse practitioner at the time. Jack had worked up as much confidence as his nerves allowed, which unfortunately led him to crash the patient's wheelchair right into her med cart.

"Hey, I'm so sorry about that! I'm a cop, but I'm terrible with shopping carts at the store..." he stammered, feeling embarrassed. Felicia gave a genuine giggle, responding, "It's okay! Is your friend okay? Is he hurt at all?" Jack almost forgot about his suspect altogether—the only thing on his mind was the beautiful nurse he had just met.

"He'll be alright, I'm sure of it," Jack had replied, managing to regain his composure. It was a fond memory, and he'd held onto it ever since that day, eventually gathering enough courage to ask Felicia on a date, albeit reluctantly.

With a shake of his head, Jack returned to the present and refocused on his usual cases and their updates. Today would be one of those slower days, which theoretically meant he could catch up on paperwork. He also often used such times to help organize police fundraisers and community events.

The day passed, and work finally ended. Jack headed home to prepare for his dinner with Felicia. Not much was needed to look nice, but he still put in the effort as a sign of devotion to hygiene and being a gentleman.

He turned on the shower but noticed Skipper looking for attention. He threw the ball around for about ten minutes, giving Skipper a good petting. Afterward, he got undressed and took a much-needed shower. Jack had to stay fit because much of his job involved driving and sitting, and he worked in Canada's largest city, where a run-in with a crackhead or a roid-raging idiot could happen at any moment. It had happened before, and he was determined to avoid any similar situations. He typically mountain biked for a few hours four to five times a week and lifted weights three times weekly. As a result, he was toned, with impressive arm muscles, though he had put on a bit of a belly over the years, especially since the pandemic in 2020, when a lot of police work went online, and many meals were limited to takeout.

His bathroom was set up perfectly for a clean bachelor lifestyle. The shower had sleek, black shelves stuck to the wall. He'd recently remodeled his mirror and sink, and it felt like shaving at the Ritz. His shower curtains were Transformers-themed, and a waterproof Bluetooth speaker was suction-cupped to the wall, providing his favorite tunes. Jack even treated himself to designer towels and scented candles from Costco, which he bought in bulk. To top off his "man bath" décor, Jack added lots of framed, pornographic photos, because why the fuck not?!

He quickly soaped up and skipped his usual jam session in the shower to save time. After drying off, he shaved, then spritzed on a bit of cologne—just enough to leave her senses tingling. He gave his puppy a final pet goodbye, then headed to the garage to make his way to the meetup spot.

They planned to meet up at Front and Spadina before going to Earls. On their first date, Jack decided to avoid any alcoholic drinks, wanting to impress her with his natural charm.

"So Jack, when did you get bumped up to homicide from constable, if I may ask?" Felicia inquired.

"Well, I started on the force about nine years ago at Division 32 as a traffic cop. I put in my best efforts for a year and five months, then got prompted to cruiser constable. I stayed on patrol for about seven years before they moved me up to homicide detective—after vigorous amounts of studying for the psych test they administer for the homicide unit." Jack sighed, a little out of breath.

"Well, I just finished my fourth-year degree in human sciences and nursing at the University of Toronto, but that's boring talk," she said, grinning. "Let's discuss what we both like...sexually?"

Jack's jaw dropped, then he smirked. "Well, like...what we enjoy in general, or kinks themselves?"

Felicia blushed a tiny bit, glancing away as the front door slammed behind a new arrival. "We could start with kinks, sure, why not!"

They quickly became absorbed in their conversation, lost in each other's words as the evening dipped into the night. Stars sparkled in the sky, and a half-moon cast a soft glow across the dark streets.

"Honestly, Felicia, I haven't had fun like this in a long time. Being a cop can really suck the fucking life out of you!" Jack admitted.

She looked down and replied slowly, "I know what you mean. In university, they had us students practice our skills in simulated situations with real actors, and some of them were so good they almost made me cry!" They both burst into laughter.

Jack checked his phone and noticed a few missed notifications. The new sheriff had emailed him expressing concern over Jack's previously impeccable attendance record and cautioning him that it would be a shame for it to go to waste. Oddly enough, the message continued with a rambling anecdote about her relationship struggles, describing it as a "jack-o-lantern" of harmony and disarray.

He skimmed through all his emails and then put his phone away, wanting to enjoy the evening with his date. Jack had an odd kink he liked with women; it involved roleplay, where he preferred to be submissive.

Felicia had gorgeous eyes, a perfectly shaped nose, and lips that complemented her face beautifully. She had an hourglass figure and was incredibly intelligent, yet a bit gullible when it came to her belief in "true love."

She was Latina, with a gentle speaking voice. Born in Ohio, USA, and raised in Alberta, Canada, her dual citizenship came in handy, especially for Black Friday shopping in the States. A way to save money from Canada's Harper-era taxes.

Passionate about her work but laid-back at heart, Felicia enjoyed board games and had a quirky hobby of collecting coins. Overall, she was cute, endearing, and charming in her own way.

The date went exceedingly well. They chatted and bonded over various topics. By the time midnight rolled around, they exchanged goodbyes, told each other what a great time they'd had, and shared a kiss. Just then, a boy nearby started laughing and pointed at them, shouting obnoxiously, "COOTIES!"

Morning came. Before he knew it, Jack's ringtone was blaring in his ear. He had fallen asleep with his phone beside his face from all the texting he and Felicia had done.

"Jack, come to the station immediately—something awful happened!" blurted the sheriff. Jack sprang out of bed, ignoring his usual hygiene routine in a rush. Half-dressed, with his wallet in his mouth, phone in hand, and keys around his neck, he sprinted out the door and nearly tripped on the stairs of his shabby apartment building.

Speeding with his lights on, Jack wondered what could possibly be so urgent for the sheriff to wake him like that. He pulled into the station parking lot, swiped his card, quickly parked in the handicapped spot, rushed to the entrance, and got into the elevator. He was sweating profusely and muttered to himself, "This better be fucking good."

As the elevator doors opened, Jack saw the entire force standing around, all with downcast eyes. Chantelle walked up to Jack and quietly told him that the coroner had passed away. The room was filled with whispers and even some quiet sobbing.

The funeral was to take place at the church the coroner had favored. Something felt off. Jack's intuition—usually spot-on in cases—was tingling. This wasn't just a simple goodbye; it felt like the beginning of a mystery, the kind of feeling he often got when he stumbled upon his first clue.

Time had passed—about three weeks—and the sheriff appointed a new coroner. Jack didn't really enjoy working with Chantelle either; it wasn't because she was a lesbian, but rather because of her attitude and the energy she exuded whenever he stood near her.

The new coroner's name was Frank Disten, a somewhat eccentric figure flown in from Boston. Chantelle reassured everyone that she knew Mr. Disten well and that everything was under control.

Jack thought it might be helpful to establish some rapport with the new coroner since they'd be working together closely on homicide cases.

During lunch on Monday, he invited Frank out for coffee.

"Listen," Frank replied, "I understand we'll need to work together and communicate, but I'm very anti-social and a bit of a hermit, so thank you, but I'll have to decline."

Jack shrugged. "Well, that's fine. I just thought I'd be nice and offer."

Chapter 6:
Drunken Aftermath

Shelia wasn't too thrilled that her mother was now publicly intoxicated in the Denny's restroom, hitting on the waiter, who was genuinely concerned for her well-being. Shelia, however, was just happy to be away from her lying, piece-of-shit, soon-to-be-ex-gay husband.

Shelia took a deep breath, stood in front of the ladies' restroom, and sternly began to tell her mom that she wasn't going to tolerate her drinking inside the bathroom and flirting with the waiter through the door. "Mom, this is embarrassing. We need to go home. Honestly, this is the stupidest thing you've ever done in front of me and with me in my entire life. I'm not screaming because I understand what addiction can do to the mind, but I swear to God, if you don't clean yourself up, I will bust this goddamn door down and pull you by your hair to the car!"

Shelia was starting to hyperventilate. After a few moments of silence, she heard the toilet flush and the tap run for a mere minute before the door finally unlocked. Out came Peggy, her shirt a little unbuttoned and disheveled. She gave her daughter a nasty but ashamed look and mumbled, "Let's go home, sugar cake. Can we not talk about this until I feel better?"

As the two walked out of the diner, they both took a moment to take in the scenery. Shelia was just relieved that this incident hadn't escalated further.

The traffic was somewhat congested; it was a long weekend in Arlen, Texas. Shelia thought carefully about how she was going to apologize to her husband and reflected on how terrible it must have been for him to hide that secret for all these years. She felt sadness sinking in, realizing she would be a single mother at 49, out of shape and out of touch with what's trendy. Nonetheless, she had to focus on her mother right now.

It hadn't been clear to Shelia before, but now she was beginning to see that her mother had struggled with alcoholism, possibly in secret, since Shelia was a child.

She pulled out her phone as she sat in the car parked in the driveway, watching her mother struggle to unlock the front door. Shelia started to dial her ex-husband but then realized she hadn't checked in with her only child. She dialed her son, Simon, and let it ring through to voicemail. She left a caring message, planning to send a follow-up text later that night.

Next, she dialed her soon-to-be ex-husband, Ginovvi. The phone rang twice, and then Doug—oddly—picked up.

"Hey, Shelia. How are you doing?"

Shelia felt awkward and hung up. She wasn't ready to talk to her husband's new lover, especially after nearly 20 years of marriage. Frustrated, she figured she could confront her husband when she returned to Toronto.

Meanwhile, her mother had given up on trying to open the front door and had decided to lie down in the front yard—like any typical drunk denied entry to her own home. Shelia opened the car door, speaking with a mix of concern and sympathy.

"Mom, just come on inside. I'll open the door for you. Give me the keys; my set doesn't have a house key, remember?"

Peggy slowly raised her head and muttered some jumbled sentences Shelia couldn't quite understand, then tossed the keys onto the lawn before letting her head fall back down onto the patch of grass. It was mostly shaded, giving her a cool spot to rest in her drunken state. As Shelia picked up the keys from the garden bed, a small spark of hope flickered in her mind. She remembered her old dream of opening a shop that sold plants, coffee, and little knick-knacks. But then she snapped back to reality as her mother started yelling at flies that were landing on her face.

The night came and went, and by 7:30 AM, Sunday morning, Shelia had just woken up and headed downstairs to make herself breakfast and coffee. When she entered the kitchen, she found Peggy already sitting at the counter, sipping black coffee.

"Shelia, I'm so sorry you had to see me like that, honey. I feel so awful and stupid," Peggy said. "I was going to mention it when you pulled up at Denny's, but I thought this whole gay husband incident might be putting too much pressure on you, and my problem would just send you overboard. I thought I had the strength to resist, but the more I thought about the taste, the more control I lost. I had been sober for over two years until this. When you were a child, I was able to hide it well, thanks to you being in school and busy with sports. How are you feeling? Did you sleep well?"

Shelia found it strange to see her mother hung over, eyes hollow and brimming with regret. Nonetheless, she sat down, took a deep breath, and thought carefully about how to respond.

"Mom, I know it must have been hard for you to get up this morning—and probably a lot of mornings when I was younger," Shelia began. "But do you think this is going to be an issue going forward? I don't mean to sound harsh, but I have enough on my plate right now with the divorce proceedings, not to mention my newly gay ex-husband and how his life might unfold with our only son. Now, I also have to plan how I'm going to tell my friends why I left. I just hope no one finds out too quickly that I married a gay man who was cheating on me. It's Toronto, and I know the city doesn't have a small-town vibe, but Ginovvi has a lot of friends around town. If he starts parading around with his husband, my friends will be furious that I didn't come to them with this kind of shit—or they'll think I'm pathetic for not realizing it sooner."

Peggy looked extremely disappointed in herself, her face crumpling as she began to cry, bringing on a long-overdue emotional breakdown. She was overcome by her fear that her daughter would end up unhappy and alone.

"Mom, I'm sorry! What did I say?" Shelia asked, standing up quickly to embrace her mother, who was now sobbing. She held Peggy tightly, comforting her until she started to calm down. After about five minutes, Peggy finally reached for some tissues on the counter and gently wiped her tears.

"Shelia, there's something I need to tell you about your husband, something I've known for a very long time. I'm sorry I didn't tell you sooner. I hoped he would come to his senses. The night of your wedding, I caught Ginovvi making out with another man. I thought it was just the alcohol—and you know I have no issues with the gay community, so I just let it go. Your father had a similar problem but with a transgender woman. He straightened out before he passed away, so I thought your husband might do the same. He was becoming so successful, and with you five months pregnant, I didn't want to ruin everything.

"But now, I see that was a huge mistake. He chased me down that night and told me it was just the drinking, that he'd seek help for his issues, and he begged me not to tell you. He even paid off a lot of my debt. He's a good man, Shelia, just the way he was born. And that doesn't change the fact that he's your son's father. Look at Simon—how smart and kind he's becoming. You have to tread carefully now. The way you approach this will shape the way Simon sees both of you. Times are different times from when you were a kid. This happens more often now."

Shelia frowned, huffed with frustration, and pulled out a pack of cigarettes. Without saying a word, she stomped out to the front yard to gather her thoughts.

Chapter 7:
The High School Love (Simon)

After a compelling night, Simon gathered all his books off his desk, went straight down to the kitchen to prepare breakfast, and did his best to avoid his newly arranged family. He ordered an Uber to the mall, planning to leave as soon as possible. On his way there, he decided to contact his mother again after receiving no response to his previous attempts. He felt awful for her, imagining what she must be going through: her life turned upside down, needing to move to Texas temporarily to find peace. She'd always been a city girl, and life—and social norms—were so different in Texas that she would stand out like a needle in a haystack.

Meanwhile, Doug was arranging items on the kitchen counter while Simon's father rested on the couch, watching the news. His dad cleared his throat and suggested, "Hey, Simon, I thought maybe you, me, and Doug could go to a movie tonight or check out a live show?"

Simon raised his eyebrow and shrugged. "Well, I don't really want to hang out with you guys. No offense, but I already made plans with Angie. Maybe some other day!" He checked the time, eager to head out, and made for the front door, not wanting to continue the awkward chitchat with his "new" family.

When Simon saw Angie at the mall, she was dressed in a blue, sunflower-patterned dress with a '70s vibe that made her eyes shine with stunning beauty. He immediately felt nervous; she wasn't usually this dolled up at school, but of course, any sensible girl knows that when an adorable boy like Simon asks for a date, it's protocol to look her best!

"Hi, Simon, how are you, sweet cheeks?" she greeted, causing him to blush and fumble for a response. "Uh, um, I'm ok…well, somewhat okay. I told you about my dad's new boyfriend, right? As if it's not bad enough that my mom totally abandoned us—I mean, who wouldn't in this kind of scenario? Now he's trying to make family plans, like the three of us going out to the movies or dinner or some stupid crap like that. I'm just so frustrated with how he sprang this on me and made my mom go crazy."

Angie's face softened, showing genuine concern and sympathy for his situation. She glanced at her phone and said, "So, the party starts in an hour. You know I can't get crazy drunk. My mom always likes to check in when I get home. No matter how late it is, she has this weird superpower of waking up the second I walk in the door. I swear, babe, I could be like a ghost, and she'd still snap out of her sleep and ask how my night was."

Simon burst out laughing. Angie wasn't one to dress up often, so whenever she did, she had this way of making him feel both enchanted and amused at the same time.

They made their way to the party, discussing future college plans during the Uber ride, both smiling and laughing the entire way. As the night continued, Simon was fraternizing with classmates when he noticed Angie yelling at a boy who was way too drunk for his own good.

"Come on, sexy, just let me kiss you and show you what a better man I am than that nerd ball, Simon," the drunk boy slurred.

Hearing this, Simon was already making his way over. As the boy's words registered, rage spread across Simon's face. He spat back, "What is your fucking problem, man? Are you seriously trying to steal my girlfriend while I'm right across the room? Are you that dumb?"

The drunk then took a swing at Simon, aiming a punch at his face. Simon blocked it immediately (his dad had signed him up for karate years ago after seeing how rough high school could get). Grabbing the boy by the shoulder, Simon threw him to the ground. The crowd around them gasped, astonished by his swift moves. No one expected this from Simon, the "drama geek" usually assumed to be weak and non-confrontational.

"Don't ever come near me or my girl ever again, you stupid piece of shit!" Simon shouted, brushing himself off. He looked over to see Angie blushing, her cheeks red as a rose.

"Wow, Simon," she said. "I've never seen you so assertive and protective. It's, uh…it's really got me going. Why don't we go upstairs?" Angie then led him upstairs to one of the bedrooms, which she had already made sure was free, thanks to help from friends she'd been texting throughout the night. Once inside, she turned and pushed Simon onto the bed, sliding her hands under her dress to unhook her bra, setting an intimate mood.

"Angie, this is…weird. I just beat up some guy for you, and there are so many people around. Wouldn't this be better at my dad's house?" Simon hesitated, aware of how close they were to a crowd.

Angie paused, remembering that Simon's mom no longer lived with him. "Simon, I want this now more than ever. There's no turning back, you strong, sexy little nerd!"

Simon was turned on after that comment, and seeing her half-naked, he sat up on the bed and began to take off his shirt and pants. He was aware that he might not get a moment like this again. Angie hopped on top of Simon's bare legs and started to rub his underwear—white briefs, of course, coming from a wealthy family. She could smell his sweat and feel his heart racing. For Simon, this was a moment he'd long imagined, and he felt an overwhelming happiness as the night unfolded into his first intimate experience with the girl he cared so much about.

Chapter 8:
Policing

Jack started heading towards the station on another beautiful day in Toronto. He wanted to get ahead of his workload, as he intended to take some time off soon to vacation with his potential new girlfriend.

When he arrived and reached the main level, he saw the chief being briefed by the press on her actions to combat organized crime within the metropolis. She seemed very formal, especially for a newly appointed police chief in a department that had faced many issues in the past. Nonetheless, Jack continued on, inquiring about certain city traffic cameras in the station's Visual IT department. Some murders were foolishly committed in broad daylight or at night on busy streets, which gave him a few leads to follow.

After reviewing CCTV footage, Jack found some promising evidence of a murder that took place near a bar on the Danforth, a common, bustling street in Toronto known for its culture. He headed back to his office to process the information further.

On his way back down to the processing area, he passed Chantelle in the lobby, who had just finished her briefing with the press. She seemed uneasy. Jack didn't stop to talk, continuing his journey to Pearson airport, where another stabbing had occurred, leading to the victim's death in transit to the emergency room.

As he arrived at the airport, ahead of his cruiser, he noticed real estate tycoon Ginovvi Radsonatti stepping out of a black Cadillac Escalade with his business partner. They exchanged a few words before something happened that blew Jack's mind. They kissed. All Jack could think about was the beautiful family Mr. Radsonatti had with that Shelia woman. Ginovvi and his wife were featured in countless billboard ads and TV commercials.

Jack wondered what Ginovvi was doing, kissing his business partner on the lips. Remaining discreet, Jack stayed parked behind the Escalade and rolled down the passenger window slightly. Ginovvi went inside the airport while Doug (the elusive one no one ever sees) remained outside making some calls. After about five minutes, Doug gave an odd smile at Jack, who managed to smile back.

Finally, Jack parked, made his way to the airport security, and requested access to the footage from the night of the stabbing. He was fortunate enough to catch a clear glimpse of the suspect's face on the video and secured a USB drive with the footage, hoping it would lead to some valuable clues.

As he prepared to leave, he noticed the two business partners, Ginovvi and Doug, holding hands as they boarded a first-class flight to Vancouver for a vacation. Jack didn't dwell on it any further.

Chapter 9:
First Class And No Ass; Doug

Ginovvi looked happy, while Doug was visibly disgusted by his so-called fiancé's behavior. Doug had no idea about the plan that was about to unfold.

They landed in Vancouver after hours of drinking and chatting with other first-class passengers. During the flight, Doug managed to pay a few people who would ensure that everything was handled properly.

Upon arrival, Ginovvi received an email from his corporate lawyer confirming his wife's signed divorce agreement. She was only requesting $2,000,000.00 and the Toronto home they shared with their son. Ginnovi, thrilled, practically jumped for joy at Vancouver airport in a modest, middle-aged manner. Turning to his new fiancé, he announced that they could finally wed now that his wife had signed the divorce papers.

Doug smiled. "Well, Ginovvi, I think we should wed on the cruise with this wonderful news!"

Ginovvi grinned back, slurring slightly with whiskey on his breath. "I agree completely, babe."

Doug internally cringed at the thought of spending the rest of his life with this man but managed to keep a pleasant smile for show. They made their way to the cruise ship boarding docks, flashed their presidential suite tickets to the Prince

Cruise staff, and waved at their personal butlers to escort their luggage aboard the luxury cruise.

Ginovvi couldn't have been happier—and neither could Doug, as the final key component of his plan had succeeded without a hitch.

Chapter 10:
The Return of Momma

Shelia had prepared herself to return to Canada, ready to face her demons and ensure her son was in good hands. She packed her bags and arranged for her mother to enter a detox program and sign up for rehab in Arlen, Texas. It cost her a significant amount, but she felt somewhat responsible for her mother's relapse and believed she would bounce back.

On the flight back to Toronto, Shelia prayed that her soon-to-be ex-husband would respect her request for the house in the divorce and not be there when she arrived. She ordered several drinks during the flight and ate a gourmet meal while mulling over how to explain everything to Simon. She wasn't entirely sure herself how things would unfold.

Upon landing in Toronto, she texted her son, letting him know she would be home shortly and asking if he could set aside some time to speak with her alone. She also asked if he knew where his father was. He replied quickly: "Dad's gone with his new boyfriend on a cruise."

Shelia sighed, feeling a mix of relief and frustration. On one hand, she was glad they wouldn't be in the house when she returned and would make sure of it. Sad that her once soulmate was now with another man., Shelia felt a complicated mix of emotions. It wasn't that she had an issue with her husband being gay; rather, it was the feeling that her entire life had almost seemed like a lie.

Determined to move on, she resolved to focus on talking to her son and making new plans for her living arrangements. She intended to sell the house and had already looked at real estate agents to list it, planning to move forward without Gino's consent—she didn't give a fuck what he had to say anymore. Shelia hailed a taxi, gave the driver her address, paid in cash with a tip, and settled in for the ride. She knew exactly what to pay from years of family vacations. On the way home, she flipped through a small photo book she kept in her purse—a bittersweet reminder of the family she once cherished but now felt had become a source of stress.

When she arrived, she typed her access code into the gate, and the brass rails opened. As she made her way to the front door, Simon opened it and hugged her tightly.

"Oh, Simon, I'm so sorry this happened right before you were about to graduate. I hope you're not mad at me for stepping away for a few days," she said.

Simon took a deep breath, struggling to keep his emotions in check. "Listen, Mom, I kind of knew Dad was like this all these years. I just thought he would snap out of it. Anyway, I'm glad you're back. There's something I want to tell you—I have a girlfriend, and her name is Angie."

Shelia smiled, barely surprised by his confession. "That's wonderful, honey! Angie is such a bright, beautiful girl with an incredible personality. I always thought you two would become a couple—I just didn't want to jinx it."

After settling in, Shelia prepared dinner. She briefly wondered about Gino's whereabouts but quickly dismissed the question. She was here for her son, not for her selfish husband.

Shelia prepared some burgers on the BBQ for herself and her son. Since she wasn't familiar with barbecuing, she asked Simon to light the grill. As she stood by, watching the AAA patties sizzle, her mind wandered. She imagined the public's reaction when they inevitably found out about Gino's newfound love. Pushing that thought away, she checked her bank account on her phone and was surprised to see an additional million dollars that she hadn't expected. She assumed it was a payout from Gino, perhaps an attempt to persuade her to agree to a quick divorce deal, though she hadn't signed any papers or contacted her lawyer yet.

"Simon, the burgers are ready," she called out.

Simon rushed down the stairs like a starved child and sat at the white marble island countertop with its dark brown base.

"Mom, what's going to happen to us? Where will Dad live? Will we have to move?" he asked, wide-eyed.

Shelia, closing the deck door that led to the BBQ and the sparkling blue pool, turned to her son. "Well, Simon, we're not going anywhere. After your father told me about his new boyfriend, I had a meltdown in the restaurant. I threw bread in his face, stormed out, and had to be escorted out by security. Then, I went straight to the airport and flew home."

She pondered her recent actions, considering the possibility of a fresh start away from the city, perhaps even in the countryside. Or possibly moving to the U.S.

She found herself wondering when Ginovvi had started to feel this way and how long he had kept his secret.

Reflecting on the betrayal, she still couldn't believe they'd chosen her favorite restaurant to break the news. As she ran through her mental task list for reclaiming her home, she made plans to remove the tacky artifacts and gaudy nude male statues she'd never truly noticed until now. She even wanted to repaint the bedroom and buy a new bed, worried about her husband's potential indiscretions.

She felt a shift in her personality—a new coldness coming to life. It was as if the old Shelia had stepped aside, and in her place was someone more detached, a woman who was done with pretending. She would rebuild her social life, even if her husband's "coming out" became the latest gossip among her friends. At that moment, she decided she was ready for whatever came next.

Shelia headed to the boutique in Yorkdale shopping center, a mall in Etobicoke primarily meant for the upper-middle class. Otherwise known as Yorkdale, it rarely saw any criminal activity, and panhandling was strictly prohibited. After some thought, however, she decided to take her shopping trip to the IKEA outlet near the 401 Highway, where the pricing would be more appropriate for her plans. Shelia was ready to replace many items she now deemed unfit for her home with her only son.

As she sped down the highway in her BMW SUV, she briefly debated drinking away all her problems. She had been holding in all the pain from the breakup since it happened in that downtown Toronto restaurant. But she knew she needed to stay strong for her son and her future. Alcohol, she realized, could make things worse quickly; she remembered her mother cycling through multiple boyfriends during her childhood. Shelia never pictured herself feeling so low that she'd even imagine turning to a life of substance use.

Returning to the present, she thought about what bedding to buy, given that she'd been sleeping on velvet sheets for the last 15 years of her marriage. A troubling thought crossed her mind: Had he slept on that bed with other men? After a frustrating 20-minute drive through traffic on the Allan Expressway due to an accident, she finally parked and decided to check out the newly renovated Willam Sonata store as well. She was definitely in a spending mood, with all the extra credit cards that hadn't been canceled yet.

Shelia wondered if the sudden, substantial deposit she had noticed earlier was just a small portion of a larger payout. It seemed unusual, given her husband's meticulous handling of legal and financial matters. He always ensured every step was well-documented, especially when it came to notifying others of payments.

While shopping at Yorkdale, she received a text from Doug, her estranged husband's boyfriend. The message included photos of Doug and Ginovvi on a boat, and Shelia felt a surge of rage. How could that "ugly office man" flaunt affection while she was clearly suffering? Initially, she deleted the message in anger, but a moment later, she recovered it, realizing it could benefit her down the line.

She had finished all her shopping at the mall and was heading to her car when she realized she had forgotten the bed sheets and new comforters. She was so distracted from all the pain she wasn't experiencing from unwanted attention and lingering trauma thoughts that her mind wandered back to when she first met Ginovvi and when she found out she was pregnant with Simon. She smiled as she remembered the first moment when she thought she might finally have the family she always dreamed of.

She came back to reality and decided she would take the scenic route home instead of the busy highway. She planned to listen to her favorite podcast and think about how she would approach the whole makeover—whether she would do it herself or leave the stress to the renovators she would hire. In the end, she decided to save money and do all the renovations herself. That way, she could keep herself busy and not dwell on what she would have to prepare for when her husband returned and she would have to address him in person.

She finally reached the halfway point and saw her phone buzz on the car dashboard. Her son's text stated that he was going out with his girlfriend and wouldn't be returning until the next morning. She thought that was a bummer, as she kind of envisioned them playing card games and drinking a little while painting and redoing the bedroom. Shelia was never one to complete projects on her own, but she decided sometimes it was nice to try new things.

As she made her way up the driveway, she noticed a little note sticking out of the shed door near the garage. Due to her

OCD, she had to pick it up. She immediately recognized it as Doug's handwriting. After her husband had worked with this man for about ten years, she had seen enough of his writing to recognize it instantly. She wondered why the note explained a list of to-do tasks, written in red, and seemed rushed. She could only read two tasks: that Doug must swoon his partner and then prepare for the eloping. She thought nothing of it, shrugged, and scraped the little piece of paper, returning to bring in all the paint and new supplies, the bedding, and a few items she wanted to try and feel sexy in—for herself and no one else.

Simon had left a note on the entrance table for his mother, saying that he would "return by no later than 11 AM." When she came home, the house seemed quiet: an empty living space and a lack of snacks all over the place. She felt a little lonely.

She started with the bedroom, stripping the bed of all the sheets she and her husband had slept on year after year. The smell of Bounty laundry detergent wafted into the air as she tossed them into the garbage bin she had readied for redecorating her new, private master bedroom. Turquoise was the color she had chosen for the walls, with a light shade of purple to accent them. She decided that new rugs that displayed aquatic life were her style. She planned to decorate the walls with indigenous women's art, and photos of her and Simon would fill the space as the years went on.

Chapter 11:
The Find

Simon was out and about with Angie and thought to himself that since his father was on vacation, it might be fun to snoop through his father's office. He knew the code and had stolen a set of keys before he left the house while his mother was busy destroying the bedroom and re-decorating the entire layout of the interior.

"Hey, baby girl, want to snoop through my father's office? He and his new boyfriend are on vacation. Let's see what we can fuck up!" Simon said.

Angie made a concerned smile. "Simon, don't you think we'll get in trouble? Isn't this breaking and entering?"

Simon laughed and responded quietly, "No, Angie, it's my dad's office, and my mom won't care. She pretty much hates him. You should have seen her destroy the bedroom and repaint it. She was shouting the entire time. I won't lie. It was funny how she kept cursing and swearing."

Angie giggled, and they proceeded into the office. Simon went straight for his dad's office and riffled through paperwork while Angie pretended to be the secretary at the front desk. She picked up the phone and mocked the secretary, stating she worked for rich, cocky fucks at real estate for cock suckers, and Simon burst out laughing.

Simon found nothing of interest and proceeded to Doug's office. He tried to open it, but it was locked.

"Huh? That's weird. This door is never locked. I've done this many times before, Angie, and that's why I wasn't worried. But Doug's office has never been locked, and this doorknob is new. Why would he change the doorknob? How did he do this without my dad knowing? Maybe he knows I come here from time to time," Simon said.

Angie came to inspect the knob. She knew a trick for picking locks, so she pulled out her tweezers and her nail file and began to work her magic on the knob. After about two minutes, she successfully opened the door and said, "And presto!"

The two curious teens entered the office with caution, as if there were lasers waiting to fire their brains. There were many little Star Wars figurines and enlarged photos in frames of Doug selling large properties that covered the wall. A black office chair, which clearly cost a fortune, sat behind a mahogany desk piled with lots of files. There were also tons of pens without lids inside a pencil holder.

Simon started opening some of the drawers on the desk, and the bottom left one was locked.

"Angie, this drawer is locked too. Can you pick that one?" he asked.

Angie came over and looked. "Simon, I can't pick this lock. It's too small. He's definitely hiding something. I wonder what it could be?"

Simon smirked and thought of countless possibilities. Angie started to kiss Simon, but he interrupted her.

"Angie, we've got to be careful. The secretary sometimes comes here to do work she's behind on. Let's go home. I'm getting tired anyway. You can sleep over. Let's not mention this to anyone because if we tell my mom, she'll want us to fuck up the office even more—knowing her and the rage she's experiencing," Simon said.

Angie laughed. "Woman, eh?"

Simon joined her in a burst of laughter, and the two left the office, locked everything up, and made sure not to leave any tracks of their criminal experience behind.

They decided to grab a late-night shake at Shake Shack in downtown Toronto. Simon got a banana shake, and Angie decided on a strawberry cream shake. Once seated, they began to speak about what Doug could be hiding.

"Well, Angie, I don't know what he could possibly be hiding. It's probably gay porn or a marriage license for the two. My mother has access to those offices, so I imagine they thought ahead and locked it up where she wouldn't find it," Simon said.

Angie looked amused. "Simon, what if it's something darker than that? What if he has all your old Tamagotchis because he kills his plants and needs practice?"

The two burst out laughing, sighing with comical relief from the whole situation.

They made their way home after a nice long hug and a kiss goodbye at Dundas Station. The school year was almost over, and they wanted to be ready.

Chapter 12:
The Landing

Ginovvi and Doug finally finished their cruise on July 13th, 2024, and were officially married by the ordained minister aboard the ship. They had been at sea for a week, thoroughly enjoying themselves, and returned to the office the following Monday.

On the ride in, Ginovvi wondered why Doug was quiet and on his phone the entire time. Ginovvi walked into the office and greeted his secretary as she was setting up the espresso maker. Doug asked her to go grab a specific kind of espresso from the store. By the time she had left, Doug had settled into his office, and Ginovvi attempted to use the coffee maker side of the Nespresso machine. Suddenly, everything went black.

911 Operator: "Hello, do you need police, fire, or ambulance?"

Doug: "I need an ambulance. My business partner isn't breathing. He slipped and hit his head on the coffee table. There's blood everywhere!"

911 Operator: "Okay, what's the address you're calling from?"

Doug: "595 Bay Street Suite. Should I try to resuscitate him or anything?"

911 Operator: Help is on the way. Stay with him and make sure first responders can access the office."

Doug: "My secretary is waiting downstairs to wave them down. I'm so scared. I don't want him to die!"

Ginovvi Radsonatti was pronounced dead at the scene by Toronto paramedics. The chief of police happened to be in the mall shopping when she saw the stretcher being rushed to the elevators and ran to help. Detectives were called in to rule out foul play. Jack O'Connor received the call at 11:03 AM on July 15th, 2024, and arrived at the scene. It seemed like a waste of gas, being two blocks away, but he needed his materials and police laptop.

He entered the lobby of the real estate office, which had high-end chandeliers, marble coffee tables, and luxurious chairs. He then found a man lying on the floor with a pool of blood seeping from his body. The coroner's deputies were loading the body onto a stretcher, and he saw Chantelle there, talking with Mister Foreheights.

"Chantelle, what a surprise to find you here. Why has the body been moved? I need to assess the entire scene to rule out homicide!" Jack side.

Chantelle glanced at her notepad. "Jack, everything's fine. I was able to find that Mister Radsonatti slipped on some coffee, spilled it on the floor, and smacked his head on the glass end tables."

Jack was astonished she was able to deem it so quickly a slip-and-fall. He would wait for the coroner's report to finalize this scene.

"If it's alright with you, I want to speak to the coroner once he's finished his report. I suppose if you feel it's a slip-and-fall, I'll just go back to my office and pick up the report later tonight. Being you're not on duty, Chief Chantelle," he replied.

She smiled and replied, "That's quite alright with me O'Connors."

He turned to exit the office and saw the crime scene deputies continuing to photograph the scene. He stepped over the coffee spill and noticed the glass tile flooring. He thought how easy it was to slip into those fancy-dress shoes these realtors wear to sell houses, with no grip and all show.

As he pushed open the doors, he noticed the cup on the floor was clean. Odd. He made his way back to the police station on College Street, briefed the paperwork he had, and hours passed by. Finally, at 5:00 PM, he finished and went down to the morgue to speak with Frank. The coroner's report indeed stated that Ginovvi had bled to death from the impact on the glass end table—so sad and truly tragic.

Despite the report, Jack still felt something was off. So, he decided the next day he would speak to Doug himself, catching him off guard. Seeing as Chantelle was there, he couldn't do this on the clock. Something about her presence didn't sit right either.

Chapter 13:
The Burial

July 27th, 2024, at St. James Cemetery, Ginovvi Radsonatti was set to be put to rest. Simon couldn't bear the fact that his father was gone. He didn't understand any of it and was heartbroken from the whole situation, bawling his eyes out with Angie holding his hand tightly. His mother was under a veil and seemed rather calm, but every few moments, you could catch her using a black handkerchief to wipe her tears. They lowered the coffin, and the violins began their symphony.

It was a sunny and humid day in the northeast corner of downtown Toronto, and everyone was using battery-powered fans or mini towels to wipe the sweat from their foreheads. Shelia came close to Simon, held him tightly, and began sobbing herself. At that moment, she regretted all the nasty things she had ever said to Gino.

Doug walked over and spoke, "Shelia, Simon, I'm so sorry for your loss." He was emotionless, which was off-putting to Shelia. Nonetheless, she sobbed more and managed to respond, "Doug, I know we weren't on the best of terms, and I'm sorry for the restaurant incident. How are you holding up?"

Doug looked like he had seen a ghost. He was as pale as could be. "Well, honestly, I was raised in a very homophobic family and taught that men don't cry. So, I guess that tradition is still alive in me. I'll manage, but I miss him dearly. His life was cut short, and it's not fair!"

Shelia agreed and nodded. After that, Doug again expressed his condolences and headed toward the black car with the chauffeur waiting for him. He got in the car and took off. Shelia looked at Simon and decided they would go out for lunch instead of the funeral-catered lunch waiting at the house on cemetery property. Shelia felt like a submissive, as she wasn't in the mood to wait for food to be served to her. She had a heavy appetite from all the crying and strong emotions tied to her recently divorced husband and the father of her only child.

They found a subway on Parliament Street, down the road from the burial, and both ordered meatball subs in honor of Gino. Simon started the conversation with a light topic of his grandmother's state and welfare.

"So, Mom, how's cowboy grandma?" he asked, a nickname he had for Peg since he was a young boy.

"Well, grandma's fine," Shelia replied. "I'm sorry I've been so quiet and distant these past few weeks. You must think I'm a horrible mom for up and leaving you when they announced their engagement. Simon, the thing is, when you've been married as long as I have been to your father, and you find out the whole time it's been a secret waiting to pop, you question every part of your life. I can't say I'm at all satisfied with his passing. I'm traumatized and truly devastated by it all. But one thing I do know is we can now work on the life we have in the present. Do you think you and I can get along fine? Your father left me two million, to be exact, in the divorce. Some of it is tied up in the business, but I know he had a will, and I know he left some more money for us. If I'm not mistaken, he had a pricy life insurance policy, but now that he's married to that buffoon, I'm not too sure what's going to happen anymore."

Simon continued to eat his sub and, after swallowing, spoke.

"Well, Mom, I was kind of curious. Maybe we could go on a vacation to forget about all this temporarily and spend some quality time together. And maybe Angie could come if you'd allow her to?"

Shelia smirked and sighed. "Well, you know what? We haven't had our yearly summer getaway. So why not? You're very fond of that girl. Unlike other mothers, I'd rather know her than rebel against her."

Simon raised his hands and did a mini dance, nearly shouting back, "CAN WE GO TO DISNEYLAND?"

Shelia nearly choked on her food and coughed, which turned into a very heartful laugh. She hadn't seen Simon so excited in a long time.

"Ok, fine, but we're all sharing a room, so don't even think of fucking that girl while I'm asleep. If I catch you, I'll spank your ass right in front of her!"

Simon looked scared and smiled at the same time. He had never heard his mom swear before. They finished their meals and made their way back to the church to collect Shelia's BMW.

After thanking friends, family, and distant relatives at the funeral home, Shelia and Simon strapped themselves in and made their way home. As for what their life might entail now, only God would know.

Chapter 14:
Vacation With Mickie

Simon eagerly packed his things and called Angie at the same time, nearly flying through the roof with excitement. She finally answered, and he continued to throw clothes and hygiene items into his luggage.

"Hey Simon, I just heard about your father's death, and I'm so sorry."

Simon almost forgot about it for a mere second and then went back to his rowdy state. "Angie, baby girl, WE'RE GOING TO DISNEYLAND, AND YOU'RE COMING!"

She dropped her phone in surprise and picked it up immediately. "Simon, whoa, hold on. Your dad dies, and you want me to come to a theme park? Are you processing this right?"

Simon frowned, remembering she didn't know his mother had suggested it. "No, babe, you don't get it. It was my mom's idea, and she thinks it will be good for us. She wants a distraction from our lives currently, and I can't blame her. So, what do you say?"

Angie was silent for a minute, then said, "You know what? Fuck it, why not. My plans for the summer were to volunteer for my junior year's hours but screw that. I want to have fun, and knowing your family, we won't be sleeping in the camps Disney sells. A hotel room and a bed will be nice for cuddles!"

Simon smiled and explained the rest of the details. The teens went to bed that night overly eager, as Shelia fought with customer service representatives on the phone over first-class tickets.

7 AM arrived, and Shelia was driving in her BMW while Simon sat in the back, waiting for his sweetheart to sit with him. Shelia pulled up to 10 Hogarth Street off the Danforth to pick up Angie. They drove up the Don Valley Parkway to then merge into the 401 for Pearson Airport. A great vacation awaited them.

As they checked through security, Shelia's phone started ringing. She answered after seeing "PRIVATE NUMBER" pop up.

"Hello?"

Jack was on the line. "Hello, Mrs. Radsonatti, it's Detective Jack O'Connor. I'm just following up on the death of your ex-husband if that's alright. Are you free at all today? These are just some minor questions I have. You're not in trouble; we've ruled it out as a slip and fall."

Shelia flustered. "I'm so sorry, Detective. I'm about to take off to Florida for a vacation at Disneyland. Is there any chance we can meet when I return?"

Jack figured the poor family wanted a getaway, especially Shelia. "Well, of course. Just call me when you return to the city. Have a great trip."

Shelia looked at her son and, hopefully, daughter-in-law one day. "That was weird. A detective just called wanting to ask me questions about your father. I wonder why?"

Angie didn't hesitate to react. "Honestly, your dad's new boyfriend, that Doug guy, his business partner—whatever—I get the creeps from him. My mom bought a house through your family, and he was the representative. We moved into it about two months ago, and I just got off vibes and creepy feelings from him. It was uncomfortable."

Shelia darted her eyes to Angie's and contemplated what she had just said. Shelia, too, had felt uncomfortable around Doug for years now. Thinking back, he always seemed miserable and angry.

Chapter 15:
Dining With The Devil

Jack hung up the phone and decided to schedule another date with that beautiful nurse. He chose to go to Earl's, a fancy restaurant downtown. After the day finished, he said goodbye to Janet and took the liberty of preparing for his date once he arrived home. He shaved, showered, and followed up with expensive cologne. He also cleaned up his apartment in case she wanted to come home afterward and have fun.

Skipper, eager for a walk, was waging his tail and barking at the door. Jack figured he had the time, so he grabbed the leash and took the boy for a short sniff around. Jack secured the leash, locked up his apartment, and headed for the stairway. That's when a call came in from the coroner. He quickly answered the phone.

"Hello, Frank, what do you have for me?"

Frank coughed before responding. "Well, Jack, it's a fracture to the skull and loss of blood that killed him. The loss of blood was significant enough to cause cardiac arrest. I'll email the report to you, but it seems as though it was all an accident. So, there is no need to continue investigating. I'd say close it here and move on with more important cases."

Jack stopped in his tracks on the staircase. Why was the coroner directing him to wrap up the case? It felt very unusual.

"Jack, are you still there?"

Jack returned to reality and said, "I'm not sure how you guys work in America, but here I make the call on when and what the case is ruled out as. But if that's the report, I have no reason to suspect foul play."

The phone call ended. Jack didn't know what the old fart thought he was doing, telling him what was going to happen. Maybe it was an American thing, or perhaps he thought he was part of the force. In Boston, they might run things differently. Asking for the medical coroner's opinions might have been a tradition, but Jack wasn't buying it.

He walked Skipper through the park, made it back just in time to let him in, locked up again, and headed for his Charger in the parking lot. He picked up Felicia at her condo in the east end, right on Kingston Road, and they headed downtown for Earl's.

He smiled at her. She was in an elegant, tight red dress and not too short or long at the legs, with shining black glittered heels. She couldn't appear more beautiful than she was at that moment.

"So, Mister Detective, how's work been? Better yet, how are you?" Felicia asked.

Jack grinned heavily and whispered, "My work isn't your business, foxy woman."

Felicia darted a look at him and nearly shouted, "What did you say?!"

He laughed, and so did she. After a conversation about boring paperwork and possible cases going cold (without any details being revealed), they finally found a parking spot for Earl's. The two were seated outside, with the night coming to life. Jack ordered a steak with seasoned mashed potatoes and some corn on the side, while Felicia stuck to a salad and a fancy noodle-filled beef broth soup. The meals were truly divine, and they gossiped about coworkers, laughing as if a comedy show were taking place. Everything was swell until Jack spotted, out of the corner of his eye, the chief, Chantelle, leaving with Doug, the newly widowed husband of Ginovvi Radsonatti. His hair stood up, and it felt that something was off in his mind and body.

He had to excuse himself for the night. Throwing down two $50 bills, he apologized to Felicia and made his way to his Charger. He saw the black Suburban take off, heading westbound. He started his car and quickly sped off, keeping enough distance between the Suburban and himself. He knew something was up—he could smell it.

As the black car continued, it made its way onto Lakeshore, and Jack kept one car between himself and the chief. Why was Doug with Chantelle, and what were they up to? His suspicions were running wild, and countless scenarios were playing out in his mind. They finally turned onto the Queensway, and the car stopped on Marine Parade Drive in front of a luxurious condo.

Jack parked behind a minivan, and that's when it hit him: Ginovvi was murdered. Frank was waiting there, and Doug got out of the Suburban to hand him a small envelope, thick as if thousands of dollars were inside. Jack knew something was off, and he had to act on it. He couldn't believe his eyes. He sat in his car for a few minutes before going onto the Radheights website to book a viewing for a new condo. He entered a false name and his phone number, hoping the viewing would be scheduled for a few days from now.

He wasn't going to let this slip away. There had to be a large insurance policy, and he needed to speak to Shelia immediately, without raising suspicion.

Chapter 16:
Sunny Days Always End

Simon was so worn out that he slept on the flight home while Angie and Shelia spoke on a variety of topics. They laughed and drank alcohol-free beverages in first class, including virgin Shirley temples and pina coladas. By the time they landed in Toronto, Shelia had woken Simon, and they had made their way to the plane's exit. Once they grabbed their luggage, they headed to the parking lot to get the BMW. Shelia packed everyone's suitcases into the trunk and drove Angie home, wishing her a good night as it was nearly 8 PM.

Once Shelia shut the back door, she turned to Simon to ask about his plans for the summer. She had many ideas of her own, including shopping with old friends. Simon spoke of learning Spanish and volunteering with Angie to get ahead on the high school hours needed to graduate. Shelia smiled, thinking about what a wonderful son she and Ginovvi had raised. This reminded her to call that detective back.

When they got home, they noticed the grass was dying and entered a house without hydro. "What the fuck?" Shelia exclaimed. Simon looked at his mother as she placed her hand over her forehead and closed her eyes. "Shit, I forgot that the hydro company and the rest of the utilities were in your father's name. There are probably notices in that giant pile of mail on our entrance table. Sweetie, go to bed. You look exhausted. I'll figure this out. It's way too late to get a hold of anyone right now for gas, hydro, and water. Are you hungry at all?"

Simon shook his head, thanked his mom for asking, and made his way to his bedroom, where he passed out fully clothed with the door open. Shelia giggled as she walked past him to put her luggage in her room. She then attempted to call Toronto Hydro. A representative answered and explained that she would have to come to an office and create a new account. She sighed, thanked the man, and then called the detective.

"Hello, Jack O'Connors speaking," the detective answered.

"Oh, hi, Detective. How are you? I just returned home, but my hydro and utilities have all been cut off. I've been so stuck in my own world that I didn't bother to check the mail or take care of any responsibilities. I am available, but my house isn't exactly guest-friendly at the moment."

Jack rustled around on his end. "It's okay, Shelia. I'm on my way. Please text me the address of your house. It's urgent, so we will speak as soon as possible. Is your son home?"

Shelia glanced at the staircase. "Yeah, but he's currently asleep. Why did you need to speak to him at all?"

More rustling. "No, not at this moment. Maybe another day when he's awake and more alert. I'm just heading out of my apartment now. I'll see you shortly."

Shelia texted him the address and decided to light some candles. Then she remembered that the backup generator needed to be switched on in the basement. Excited, she ran downstairs as she hated the dark. She switched it on, and the house came to life. The LED screen on the generator indicated it had two days of use left, which was more than

70

enough time to get things up and running. Shelia used the washroom, cleaned herself up, and prepared some coffee.

The gate intercom buzzed. Jack had arrived. She checked the cameras and saw a red Dodge Charger. He had given her that description, so she opened the gates. He parked in front of the garage door and exited the vehicle.

"Well, I'm glad you have power again. I don't know how you would have opened that gate without it. Hi Shelia, I'm Detective Jack O'Connor. It's so nice to meet you. You can call me Jack, though."

They shook hands, and both smiled. "Hi, Jack. Come on in. I just brewed a pot of coffee if you'd like some."

Jack took off his coat and happily accepted. Just then, Simon came bolting down the stairs.

"Mom, you got a hold of someone? The lights are back on. My TV woke me up."

Shelia grinned. "Jack, this is my son, Simon. Simon, sweetie, this is Detective Jack O'Connor. He's here to ask some questions about your father."

They shook hands.

"Wait, why? I thought Dad died from a slip and fall?"

Jack shrugged. "Well, if you don't mind, Shelia, after I'm done asking you some questions, may I speak to Simon? You both can be present."

Shelia nodded, and they sat down in the living room. Simon grabbed himself a can of root beer and sat beside his mom.

"So, do you have a gun, officer?" Simon asked.

Shelia snapped, "Simon, stop with that. You're being foolish. Of course, he has a gun. You do have a gun, right, Jack?"

Jack laughed. "Yes, of course. I left it in the car so as not to alarm you or your son. Anyhow, I'd like to start asking some questions about your ex-husband. From what I gather, he left you for his business partner, and there are certain elements that I would like to know. First question: What is the insurance policy payout in terms of your beneficiary payment?"

Shelia looked stunned and a little offended. "To be honest, I don't actually know. I received 2 million for the divorce, and this house and all that was taken care of. I completely forgot all about that. But from what I know, it's big in accidental death. Fuck, that fat turd's getting 10 million dollars. WHAT A BIRD!"

Simon burst out laughing, and Shelia gave him the look of death. Jack had to hide the fact that he, too, was about to laugh at the comment, but he kept his professionalism and continued after jotting some notes down.

"What was the relationship between you and Doug like?

Shelia frowned. "Well, he's a creep, and he always seems angry. But that being said, he was always polite to me, short conversation, nothing more than a few sentences. There was never any reason for me to talk to him."

Simon jumped in. "My girlfriend Angie said he was a creep too and that he stared at her mom's chest like two months ago when he sold them a house."

Jack's eyebrow raised. Shelia then jumped in. "Wait, do you think my son's father might have been murdered?"

Jack looked up with an emotionless expression. "I can't say, Shelia, but I feel that's possible."

She gasped and started to weep. Jack apologized and asked if she needed a moment.

"No, Jack, it's just so awful for my son," Shelia said, her voice trembling. Simon stormed off to his room, hiding his face with his hoodie. The fact upset him gravely.

"Anything you want, Jack, I'll give it to you," Shelia said, her tone soft but resolute.

Jack turned back to him after watching Simon run off and asked for the life insurance company as well as a shared bank account statement to determine how much money Ginovvi had put away. Shelia did not hesitate with any request. She grabbed all the documents she could muster up and put them in a large envelope.

Jack finished the coffee and thanked Shelia, expressing how sorry he was for her loss. She teared up a little and smiled, then asked him quietly, "If Doug did this, you get that fat piece of shit and lock him up where he belongs." She kissed Jack on the cheek and shut the front door.

Jack looked at the envelope and made his way to the car. He went inside and opened the paperwork, discovering that Ginovvi was incredibly wealthy. He had a savings account with almost 15 million dollars. This was for sure a murder, poor Gino, and Jack was determined to nail these bastards for what had happened.

Chapter 17:
Caught Him By Surprise

Doug was well-tailored for a potential client selling a very high-end condo in the heart of downtown Toronto. He made sure the water bottles were neatly arranged and ensured the Starbucks cards worth $10 each were available. He knew the client's name was George, and his wife would be coming as well.

There was a rough knock on the door, and Doug wondered who it could be. The client was supposed to inform the front desk that they had arrived. He opened the door to find Detective Jack O'Connors standing there.

"Oh, Detective! What might you be doing here?" Doug asked his tone a mix of surprise and curiosity.

Jack flashed his million-dollar smile. "Well, I had my assistant book the viewing. I'm in the market for a new place to live and thought I'd give your company a shot at impressing me."

Doug looked incredibly confused, then smiled. "Oh, your assistant booked the viewing? She must have mistakenly put you down as George brown."

Jack gazed at the refreshments and replied, "That's her husband's name. She must have been very tired. I do apologize for that."

Doug readjusted his blazer and began showing Jack around the condo. It wasn't until they reached the bedroom that Jack decided to throw an off-topic question.

"So, how long did you love Ginovvi behind Shelia's back? And when did you decide that it was time to tell her? Did you plan it all that day, or did you decide over a period?"

Doug's brows furrowed in anger, and his tone became rude. "I beg your pardon. My husband died after spilling a cup of coffee, and he was hungover. But what in the world do you think you're doing, questioning me like this?"

Jack walked around him, observing the bedroom and pretending to take an interest in the walls. "Are these walls soundproof? I like to have lots of loud sex."

Doug completely lost track of his anger and answered the question. "Well, no, but I'm sure that we could arrange to have that done. Are you truly here to buy this unit?"

Doug looked extremely annoyed and waited for Jack to respond.

"Oh, yes, I'm very interested, Jack replied nonchalantly. "But I must be leaving. I'll be in touch with you, and I will take the condo."

Doug smiled ever so lightly. "Amazing. I can prepare the documents and have everything done and sent to the bank by as early as tomorrow morning if that's alright with you?"

Jack nodded and left.

Doug picked up his phone and dialed a number.

"Chief of police."

"Hey, we have a huge problem. Your detective was just here at a condo my company owns, trying to inquire as if he was on the market to buy. It was a ruse. He was asking questions about Gino and me, and I think he might be onto us."

Chantelle spit her coffee out as she heard this. "What the hell, was he just there?"

Doug snarked back, "Yes, he was just here. I couldn't wait to make that announcement. What are we going to do? I'm sweating buckets here, you pig! You said you had it covered with that coroner's report. Why is he asking questions now?"

Chantelle felt disgusted by his language and yelled, "Listen, you tub of shit, I'll take care of it. I got this. So go back to your bullshit of a career, and let me handle this."

Chapter 18:
The Abduction

According to his secretary, Jack was called to the chief's office late at night. He worried it had something to do with the condo viewing. He walked into the office, where Chantelle was sitting behind her desk, and sat down.

"So, Jack, you like to disobey orders, huh?"

Jack's hair began to stand up. He had left his gun at his desk, and there were very few people left in the building, but he waited to see what she was going to say.

"Listen, you're not in trouble. I just want you to read this report."

As Jack began reading the file, Chantelle's phone rang. It was the loudest ringtone he had ever heard. She got up and announced she had to take the call out of the office. Jack relaxed, went through the folder, and his jaw dropped. His resignation papers. She was letting him go.

Suddenly, a black hood was put over his head, and he took a blow to the back of his head, rendering him unconscious.

Several hours had passed, and Jack awoke in a dark, underground room. He was tied up and gagged. He wiggled around, trying to figure out his position, and realized he was tied to a post of some sort.

"Oh, O'Conner, if you had just listened to me and stayed home when the investigation began, you wouldn't be in this… awful predicament. Such a shame. You were so loyal and hardworking but also too good-spirited for this division."

"You won't get away with this bullshit game you're pulling," Jack shouted, hoping somewhere, someone nearby would hear him. The ground was extremely cold to the touch, which told him they were underground—how deep? That was beyond him.

Then he saw him. The connection to it all, the mole in their operation. The missing piece to the puzzle. Chantelle, and right behind her, Frank and Doug. They had worked together to murder the poor man.

"YOU BASTARDS! You took a father away from his family and manipulated him into thinking he had found true love!" Jack spat blood.

Doug began to speak. "Want to know how we did it? You goody-good pig! I made Ginovvi change the life insurance policy and his will after marrying him. Once we got to the office the morning he died, Chantelle bashed his head in with a crowbar, held him up, and then bashed his head again on the end table and cleaned where necessary. It was such a mess, but fuck that Faggot. The company's mine. You're going to go missing and never be seen again. Nobody will ever find you here. Who's going to look in the chief's basement? Well, in a matter of time, you will never be seen again."

Doug went through his phone, then said, "Oh, you went to see Mrs. Radsonatti? I see. I guess we will have to pay her a visit. We can't have evidence lying around, can we?"

Jack struggled to get free, but it was of no use.

Chapter 19:
Shooting In The Dark

Shelia got a call from a private number again at 3:04 AM. She assumed it was the detective, but it was Doug.

"Shelia, hey, it's Doug. Are you at home? I heard your phone ring. Let me in the house now!"

Shelia panicked and hung up the phone. Someone was banging on the door. She checked the cameras and saw her husband's Rover. It was Doug. Panic and adrenaline surged through her veins. She knew Doug was here to kill her. She saw the gun in his hand.

She tiptoed through the house and ran upstairs to grab Simon. She felt in her bones that Jack was in trouble—and that she and her son would be dead if she didn't act now.

She ran upstairs and woke Simon up.

"Sweetie, listen, come with me right now. We need to leave."

Simon didn't question her. He jumped off the bed and followed his mother down the stairs, through the hallway in his pajamas. They snuck past the front door corridor and made their way to the garage. Shelia heard the front door crash down.

"Simon, get in the car, buckle your seatbelt, and pull it all the way out," she said.

Shelia started to cry as she saw her son stricken with worry. At that moment, her motherly instincts kicked in, and her face hardened with anger. She started the car, and Simon was hyperventilating. Not wanting to wait for him to hear the garage door open, she started her BMW and said, "For you, my sweet Ginovvi."

She put the car in drive, and adrenaline ran through her veins. She floored the gas peddle and drove straight through the door, smashing it to pieces. She sped out of there and saw Doug running up the driveway, shooting at the vehicle. A tail light shattered.

She turned the corner quickly and told Simon to keep his head down. She didn't know where to go. Then, out of nowhere, she saw sirens and lights flashing.

She pulled over, panicked, and got out, thanking the Lord. The cruiser door opened, and a woman stepped out of the vehicle. Simon was watching from the back seat. The officer approached, and Shelia saw a chief badge.

"Oh, thank God, chief! Please help me! My husband's business partner is trying to kill me!" Shelia cried.

Chantelle looked at Shelia with authority. "Ma'am, place your hands behind your back. You're under arrest for careless driving and possession of a firearm."

Shelia looked horrified. "What!?"

Chantelle grabbed Shelia, and Sheila screamed, "Simon, RUN! Go find Jack, just go!"

Simon jumped into the driver's seat and sped off. Chantelle let go of Shelia and radioed in a runaway vehicle. Shelia used her body weight to slam the cruiser door onto Chantelle.

"You FUCKING BITCH!" She got her taser out and took Shelia down. Now, she couldn't remember the license plate.

Chapter 20:
The Rescue

Simon didn't know what to do, so he drove somewhere safe—his dad's office building. He couldn't call the cops because he knew his mother didn't have a gun and had connected the dots: the chief was in on the murder. He remembered his mom telling him that a chief was in the building the day his dad died. He had to find Jack, and he was close to the office.

He parked the car on the sidewalk and didn't care. He ran to the building and punched in the access code. Doug didn't know he had one, so he wouldn't have changed it. Presto— he was in. He made his way to the office and broke down Doug's office door with the fire extinguisher he stole from the hallway. Once he pried open the door, he pushed the desk over. The cheap wood split open, spilling a huge pile of files.

He quickly searched through it all and found a folder labeled Murder of a Fag: Money in the Bag. "What a sick fuck," he thought. He then noticed a sticky note that stated the detective was locked up and planned to be killed. The note also said that the detective was to be finished off in the chief's basement. Simon immediately dialed 911, panicking as he told the operator about all the incriminating evidence.

Minutes later, cruisers pulled up in front of the office, and Simon was found in the front lobby. EMS was there waiting.

Officers took the file and radioed into the division to order a SWAT team to go to the chief's house.

Armored trucks were on the road in a matter of minutes, heading to the chief's home. Meanwhile, multiple cruisers located the chief and set up a roadblock, aiming guns at her car. She pulled over, and they screamed from behind their cruisers, "GET OUT OF VEHICLE AND PLACE YOUR WEAPON ON THE GROUND." It was all over.

A SWAT team was dispatched to the chief's house after deputies saw video footage of Jack clocking in but never clocking out. They knew their new chief was corrupt. The detective was freed from his ropes, and EMS arrived at the scene of the chief's car, cornered on Lakeshore Blvd, where they treated Shelia for electric shock. Shelia was later taken to Toronto General, at her request, to be with Simon. Jack was also there, waiting for her.

Doug and the chief were arrested for first-degree murder in Ginovvi's Rover after Chantelle's corruption was exposed. Word traveled fast within law enforcement. Along with the chief and the coroner, Frank was found at the chief's house, attempting to jump the backyard fence, where officers tackled him to the ground.

Jack knew in his mind he had failed to solve the case on his own. But Simon was quite the detective himself. Maybe he had a shot at becoming a great police officer, thinking quickly at that moment to go where the potent evidence lay. He certainly had a bright future. That much was sure.

Jack knew he had to repay the family for their heroic and brave efforts to stop corruption and put to rest the murder of their father and husband. Regardless of the divorce, Jack knew Shelia still cared about Ginovvi. He could tell by the way she spoke and looked when they discussed his death. Jack was going to see if Simon might be interested in becoming a police officer. He knew he had to look out for these two heroes—Shelia and Simon—so perfect, so pure. Shelia seemed more appealing than Felicia, but time would tell where life took them.

Sequel to come in 2025

THE GOLDEN HEART FAMILY